THE LEGEND OF THE DIGIDESTINED

DIGITAL DIGIMON MONSTERS ™

John Whitman

HarperEntertainment
An Imprint of HarperCollins*Publishers*

HarperEntertainment
An Imprint of HarperCollins*Publishers*
10 East 53rd Street, New York, NY 10022

HarperCollins books are available at special quantity discounts for bulk purchases for sales promotions, premiums, or fund-raising. For information, please call or write: Special Markets Department, HarperCollins Publishers Inc., 10 East 53rd Street, New York, NY 10022. Telephone: (212) 207-7528. Fax: (212) 207-7222.

ISBN 0-06-107198-6

First printing: January 2001

Printed in the United States of America

Visit HarperEntertainment on the World Wide Web at www.harpercollins.com

❖ 10 9 8 7 6 5 4 3 2 1

Part One:
DigiBaby Boom

File Island had broken into pieces.

An Evil Digimon named Devimon had used his immense power to rip the island apart.

The evil creature had been trying to destroy the seven human children who had been mysteriously transported to the island. With the help of a Champion Digimon named Leomon, the children had escaped. But they were now scattered all over a vast ocean that separated one piece of the island from another, and Leomon had been enslaved by Devimon. Worst of all, the cruel Digimon had sworn that he would still destroy the children.

One of those children, a boy named T.K., was at that moment hanging on to a bed for dear life.

The bed was fly-
ing through the air,
which would have been
really strange on Earth.
But here in DigiWorld it
didn't seem very strange at all.

But that didn't make it any
less frightening. Especially when the flying
bed suddenly plunged out of the night sky
and splashed into the cold waters of the
ocean. Sputtering for air, T.K. shouted to a
small Digimon next to him, "Ah! What's
happening, Patamon?"

"I don't know!" the little Digimon replied.
He flapped his big ears to stay afloat.

"Just when I thought this place is the
bomb it all turns creepy on me again!"

"Don't worry, I'll get us out," Patamon
said. The digital creature began to flap its
ears even harder. The flapping ears acted as
wings, lifting Patamon's round pudgy body
out of the water. Patamon grabbed T.K.,
too, and flapped harder until the boy rose
out of the water as well.

Then, with great effort, the Digimon started flapping toward the nearest piece of island.

While T.K. and Patamon struggled toward dry land, far off on the heights of Infinity Mountain, near what used to be the center of File Island, Devimon gazed down upon his two most powerful servants. Ogremon, one of the cruelest of the Evil Digimon shuffled nervously under Devimon's gaze. Beside him, Leomon stood as still as a statue. Leomon was under Devimon's spell.

The leader of the Evil Digimon stood up to his full height, standing like a tall black spike at the very tip of Infinity Mountain. He was furious because his two servants had failed to destroy the children.

"You have failed me again!" Devimon growled.

"I am sorry, Master," Leomon said, forced to obey Devimon because of the spell cast over him.

"We almost had them, Devimon," Ogremon whined. "But then just as we–*gakk!*"

Ogremon's words were choked off as Devimon reached out and grabbed him by the throat, lifting the great Digimon.

"Spare me your pathetic excuses!"

"Yes, Master, please!" Ogremon gasped. "Just put me down!"

"Very well." Devimon smiled evilly and released Ogremon. The Digimon tumbled down the side of Infinity Mountain and crashed to a halt against a pile of sharp rocks.

Devimon smiled. Ogremon had asked for that. But then the smile turned to a frown as he thought of the children again. If the legends were right, they were the Digidestined, the humans who would break his hold over File Island and destroy him forever. He could not allow that. The children must be destroyed.

2

Meanwhile, T.K. and Patamon had managed to dry themselves off near a great waterfall, where T.K. set his clothes out in the sun. Once they were warm again, he pulled them on.

"Boy, Patamon," he said. "That water was fun and all, but splashing down almost knocked my underpants off!"

Patamon laughed. "Well, it's about time you had a bath!"

Patamon's joke made T.K. think of home, and once he started thinking of home, a feeling of great sadness came over him. It seemed like years since he'd seen his own world of Earth, wherever that was. And it also seemed like a long time since he'd seen the others.

He thought of the other six children who'd become his closest friends. First there was his older brother, Matt, and his Rookie Digimon Gabumon. Then there was Tai, the brave kid who had become the natural leader of their group along with his little Dinosaur Digimon Agumon. He thought of Sora next, one of the smartest girls he'd ever met, with her birdlike friend Biyomon, and he also thought of Izzy, a kid only a little older than T.K., but with a brain that worked like a computer, who had been befriended by the Insectoid Digimon Tentomon. T.K. even missed Mimi, who was always talking about her hair and her clothes when she wasn't playing games with the plantlike Digimon named Palmon, and Joe, the oldest kid in the group, but also the one with the biggest yellow streak down his back, who was always being encouraged by his Rookie Digimon Gomamon.

T.K. felt a tear well up in his eye, and he wiped it away as Patamon looked at him. "Don't worry, Patamon," he said. "I'm not scared of being separated from the others. And being lost, and being homesick."

He burst into tears.

Patamon frowned. *Poor little T.K.—I wish I could help.* He thought of the other Digimon that he admired. *What would Biyomon do if she were here?*

Instantly, Patamon imagined little feathered Biyomon digivolving into the mighty Birdramon.

Yeah, but I can't digivolve! Patamon thought. And then he, too, burst into tears. "Waahhh! I want to digivolve! I want to fly high in the sky. I want to digivolve!"

Startled by the little creature, T.K.

stopped his own crying. "Hey," he said.

"I want to digivolve!" Patamon said again.

"To what?" the boy asked.

Patamon sniffed. "Huh?"

"What will you digivolve into?"

"Oh." Sniff. "Well, I won't actually know until I do it."

T.K.'s eyes lit up. "Oh, wow! Well, maybe you'll digivolve into something like this!" He grabbed a stick and scratched a picture of a pig into the dirt. Then he said in his best superhero voice: "Porkymon! With super-strong oink attack and the power to, um, oink!"

Patamon frowned. "Um, maybe . . ."

"Well, how about Hogmon!" T.K. said. "Super hog smell and the power to snort up enemies in a single sniff."

Patamon's frowned turned into a pout. "I

HOGMON

成熟期

想像型デジモン
タイプ
イメージ
必殺技
ヒポポタバキューム

am not a pig, T.K.!"

T.K. shrugged. "There's nothing wrong with being a pig."

"I'm sure there's not. Especially for pigs," the Digimon said. "But that's not me!"

Ding! Ding! Ding! They heard the sound of a warning bell. Following the sound through a thin line of trees, they came to a wide, empty field. Through the middle passed a bed of railroad tracks, and the gate crossing was down. Warning lights and bells went on, as though holding cars back from crossing the tracks while the train swept through.

Totally confused, T.K. and Patamon sat down to wait.

But no train came. At least, they never saw one. But Patamon felt something brush past his face.

"Maybe it's an invisible train," T.K. guessed.

"Did a train even go by?" Patamon wondered aloud. He'd been born on File Island,

and sometimes this strange place confused even him.

T.K. shrugged. "If it did it was the most silentest, most invisiblest train ever." He sighed. "Come on, let's go."

"Where?"

"I'm not sure. I guess we'll know when we get there."

Together, the boy and his Digimon pal crossed the railroad tracks and walked across the field. At the far end they passed through another line of trees with thick leaves on their low-hanging branches.

On the other side, they saw yet another of File Island's strange sites. This one was an enormous city made of children's building blocks and other colorful things. Some of the buildings looked like giant jack-in-the-box toys, while others were made of puzzle pieces. T.K. felt like he was walking into a toyland.

His face brightened immediately. "Wow, this is the best! Let's find a snack bar and get some cotton candy. Places like this always sell cotton candy."

Patamon gulped. "They make candy from cotton?"

T.K. didn't answer. He'd already run into the toy village. But the minute his foot hit the street, he found himself bouncing into the air as though he'd jumped on a trampoline.

"Whoa!" he yelled in alarm. But then he came down and bounced again, and this time he laughed.

Patamon followed after him, and together the two friends bounded down the street until they found themselves in the middle of the town square. Taking one more giant bounce, they landed on their backs in the middle of the town.

T.K. chuckled. "The streets are soft and

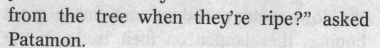

it's like they're made of marshmallows!"

____ stared up at the ___ sky for a while and at the trees that grew around the edges of the square. Toys hung from the branches like fruit. "Do you think those toys fall from the tree when they're ripe?" asked Patamon.

"I don't know." T.K. laughed.

"Well," Patamon said, jumping up and flapping his ear wings, "we can't just lie here forever, can we?"

T.K. was tired, but he nodded. "I guess we'd better keep looking around."

Patamon perked his ears. "I hear strange noises from over there."

The two walked to the far end of the square. There, they found a little park covered with grass. But instead of a playground or a fountain, the park was covered with little cradles. It looked like a hundred nannies had suddenly left their babies and walked away.

T.K. peeked inside. The creature he saw wasn't human. It didn't even look like a Digimon. It was small and black, with no arms or legs, but two pointed ears and huge yellow eyes.

"What now?"

"That's Botamon," Patamon said. "It's a baby Digimon!"

T.K. touched the creature gently and it purred. "It's so soft."

"That's because he was just born."

They looked at some of the other

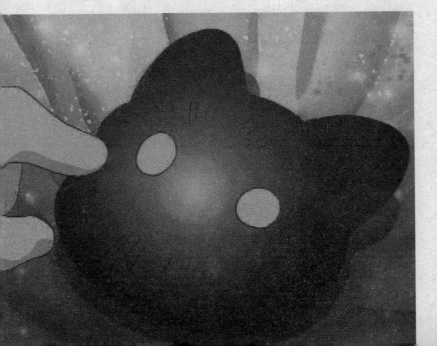

Digimon in their cradles. They were all tiny, soft, and cuddly.

Wandering through the crowd of cradles, T.K. found himself at the edge of the little beds and the beginning of a new cluster. The objects he saw now were eggs. There were dozens of them—some with stripes, others with polka dots, and all nestled in the grass of the park, keeping warm in the sun.

"What's this?" he asked aloud.

Patamon flew over to him and smiled. "That's a Digi-Egg! The egg of a Digimon!"

T.K. picked one up gently. It was about the size of his head and covered with pink stripes. "Hm, I like the stripes, but are you saying that Digimon come out of eggs like chickens?"

Patamon giggled. "We don't grow out of the ground!"

"Even Devimon?" the boy asked.

"Unfortunately," Pata- mon said, lowering his

head. As he did, he spotted a small note on the ground. He picked it up and opened it. Glancing over the Digimon's shoulder, T.K. saw two or three lines of nonsense writing.

"It's written in digi-code," Patamon explained. "It says, 'Rub gently.'"

"Rub gently?" T.K. said. "Do you suppose we're supposed to rub the egg?"

"Why not give it a try?"

T.K. rubbed the egg gently. "Maybe a digital genie will pop out." He decided that if he got any wishes he'd ask for a skateboard.

As he rubbed the egg, it started to crack.

21

3

A huge crack appeared along the side of the egg, and suddenly a tiny Botamon popped out, smiling at them with its big eyes.

"Wow!" T.K. laughed. He put the Botamon down, still surrounded by most of the eggshell. "Now we just have to find this little guy his own cradle."

"I'll look for an extra one," Patamon

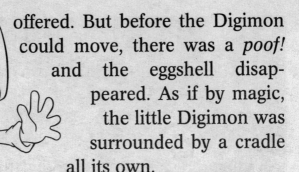

offered. But before the Digimon could move, there was a *poof!* and the eggshell disappeared. As if by magic, the little Digimon was surrounded by a cradle all its own.

Patamon blinked. "Oh, so that's how that works."

T.K. looked at his Digimon companion and realized, "You mean until just now you didn't know where you came from?"

Patamon laughed. "T.K., do you remember anything from when you were a baby?"

The boy thought about it, but couldn't recall much more than falling down or playing with stuffed animals. "Hm, okay, so it's not so easy to remember stuff from being a baby. But at least I know I didn't come from an egg!"

From the field where the cradles lay, T.K. heard one soft whimper. Then another, and another. The baby Digimon were crying!

"Hey," he said, leaning down to look at one of the babies. It was shivering and crying. "Are you all right? Are you hungry? That must be it!"

T.K. picked up the crying baby and rocked it gently, but it kept crying. And one by one, all the other babies began to cry, too, until the field was full of noise so loud it hurt T.K.'s ears.

He and Patamon ran from one cradle to another, trying to comfort the screaming creatures.

Suddenly, a voice roared at them from across the park. *"Get away from them!"*

T.K. whirled around, expecting to see a giant Digimon looming over him. Instead he saw a small creature, not much bigger than Patamon himself. The new Digimon, red with tiger stripes, growled at them.

"Intruders!" the Digimon roared. Then it

leaped into the air, shouting, "Super Thunder Strike!"

An energy bolt leaped from the Digimon's head and burned through the air. At the last second, Patamon shoved T.K. aside and the Thunder Strike bolt slammed harmlessly into the ground.

"Wow, he's really angry," T.K. said, picking himself up off the ground. He looked at the Digimon stranger, who stood on all four legs, tense and ready to strike again.

"Hey!" T.K. yelled. "You could really hurt someone doing that!"

"Of course, I could," said the newcomer

in a harsh tone. For a little Digimon, he had a powerful voice. "That's what I was trying to do."

"But why would you want to do anything to hurt us?" Patamon said.

The Digimon rushed over to the baby Digimon that T.K. had been holding. At first T.K. thought the Digimon was going to attack the baby. Instead, he picked it up gently and put it back in its crib.

"Because," the newcomer explained, "I thought you were trying to hurt my babies."

T.K. studied the creature closely. "Sure, we played with them. But what does that have to do with you?"

The Digimon snorted. "I am Elecmon, and it's my job to protect these babies. This is the Primary Village hatchling ground, a very special place where Digimon start their lives. And I am a special Digimon, entrusted with caring for each and every one of them!"

Patamon grunted. "Well, you don't have to play Mr. Big Shot and fry us!"

"I was only trying to protect my babies. Now I think this conversation has lasted long enough. You are trespassers and you have to leave."

Patamon shook his head. "Now, now, don't get all puffy."

Elecmon bristled. The hairs on his back seemed to stand on end. "Don't call me puffy!"

The two Digimon tensed up, and T.K. knew what would happen next. Digimon, even good Digimon, were born to fight, and these two couldn't resist.

4

They sprang at each other and met in midair. Patamon tried to ram Elecmon, but the striped Digimon grabbed him and squeezed, releasing some of his electrical energy at the same time.

Crying out, Patamon managed to break free. The two fighters flew apart. Patamon slammed into a wall—which seemed to be as soft as the ground.

But he wasn't ready to give up, and nei-
ther was Elecmon. They charged each other
again. This time, Patamon tried to fight
smarter. Gathering his breath, he let loose a

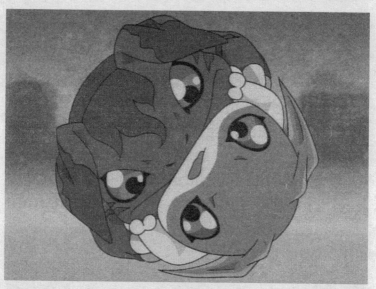

Boom Bubble, but Elecmon avoided it easily
and rammed himself into Patamon. The two
Digimon locked together and rolled around
on the grassy lawn.

"Stop!" T.K. yelled in the loudest voice he
could manage.

The two Digimon froze in place.

"Huh?"

T.K. said, "Fighting's no good for solving problems. All you did was mess up your fur and scare the babies."

"Yeah?" said Patamon. "Well, do you know what I heard? I heard that trying to act too grown up is a sign of immaturity."

"What's that?" Elecmon snapped. "If you've got something to say to me, say it to my face! Come on, out with it, you little weenie-headed two-toned pork chop!"

Patamon snarled. "Hey, T.K., can I teach this arrogant digi-toad a lesson?"

"You're the one that's going to learn something," Elecmon snapped.

"Do you guys really have to do this?" T.K. groaned.

"Yes!" the two Digimon said at once.

"Okay," said the boy, "then I've got the perfect way to settle this."

A few moments later the two Digimon

squared off, facing each other. Between them lay a rope. T.K. had arranged a tug-of-war. "This is a nicer way to settle things," the boy said. "Are you ready?"

"Ready!" Patamon said.

"Ready," Elecmon growled.

"Go!"

The two Digimon snatched their ends of the rope and started to pull. Elecmon was a bit bigger and looked stronger, but little Patamon was a stubborn Digimon, and he refused to give up. The Digimon strained and gritted his teeth. For a moment he

thought powerful Elecmon would bowl him over, but then he managed to dig his paws into the ground and give one more heave.

That last pull threw Elecmon off balance. With a strangled cry, Elecmon was thrown into the air. He landed with a soft *whoosh* in the side of a building. The building, as springy as the streets, sagged like a cookie right out of the oven.

"I did it!" Patamon yelled.

"Yeah," T.K. said. "Hey, Elecmon, are you okay?"

From high up on the side of the building where Elecmon was struggling to get out of the soft material, the Digimon called out, "Yeah, I'm okay."

Elecmon dragged himself out of the building and dropped back down to the ground. Patamon tensed, expecting the creature to be angry. But instead, Elecmon smiled. "Well, you did it, kid!" he said. "You beat me fair and square. It's my pleasure to welcome you to Primary Village."

They shook paws, and T.K. cheered. "I'm sorry about the way I acted," Elecmon said. "There's no excuse for it. But I've been so upset since the island broke apart, and I was expecting a fight. I guess I just took it out on you."

Elecmon put one arm around Patamon and used the other to wave at their surroundings. "Primary Village is wonderful. You'll like it here. I do need someone to take over someday. You'd be really good at it."

Patamon shook his head. "I'm not here to raise babies, Elecmon."

The striped Digimon looked a little disappointed. "Oh, uh, of course you're not."

T.K. interrupted. "Well, we have to get to that mountain."

He pointed off in the distance, where Infinity Mountain rose into the sky.

Elecmon gulped nervously. "You want to go up there?"

"Yep," T.K. said matter-of-factly.

"Why would you want to do that?" Elecmon asked. "You'll need special equipment to get up there. And then there's the snow—it's very cold. And there's poison ivy, and snakes and bugs—"

"And Devimon," T.K. said.

"Yeah, I was getting to that," the Digimon said quietly. "He's a very Evil Digimon."

"I know, but I have to ask him about my brother," T.K. said.

Elecmon shook his head. "He's not just going to tell you. You'll have to fight him."

"I'm not going to fight!" T.K. insisted.

"There has to be some other way," Patamon said.

"Sure, there is," T.K. said. "Remember how it felt a minute ago when we were laughing together. We have to do the same thing with Devimon."

Elecmon thought for a moment, then a spark of light filled his eye. "Say, you might be right. That's it!" He suddenly smiled. "T.K. is right. It's all about laughing and being friends. Maybe we can use the power of friendship to bring the island back to normal. I've got to go!"

And with that, the tough little Digimon bounded away through the trees.

5

Little did T.K. know, but high atop Infinity Mountain, Devimon was using his power to watch T.K. and Patamon.

Devimon said to himself, "All the Digimon have managed to digivolve except this one. I must destroy this last one before it is too late. I can't believe it's come this far. Still, as long as even one of the Digidestined remains weak, they cannot destroy me. Leomon!"

At the command, Leomon stepped forward. Devimon said, "Leomon, I leave this to you."

"Yes, Master," the Champion Digimon growled.

"What shall I do, Master?" Ogremon asked. "What task do you have for me?"

Devimon considered. "Nothing yet. But soon a battle shall rage. You must be prepared."

"I will not fail you!" the Evil Digimon promised.

Devimon laughed. "No, there will be no failure this time. I will be victorious!"

Back in Primary Village, T.K. and Patamon had spent the afternoon playing with the baby Digimons. They seemed to grow quickly once they hatched from their eggs. After spending a little time in their cradles, the babies, called Botamon, grew into larger Digimon that could crawl around and play, although they still couldn't speak.

T.K. laughed as a baby Digimon plopped into his lap and giggled. "Just think," he said, "someday you'll grow up into a huge Digimon. Maybe you'll even digivolve into something as big as Greymon or Kabuterimon!"

Standing nearby, Patamon watched his friend hold the little Digimon.

He felt jealousy creep over him. "Remember, T.K.," he said, "I'm your Digimon and someday I'll digivolve, too."

"Hm?" T.K. said. "Is that bad?"

"No, it's not!"

"Then," T.K. said, trying to understand, "you want to digivolve? Is that it?"

Patamon thought a moment. "Well, I do, I guess. But not right now. I want to stay like this and help you forever."

T.K. beamed. "Yeah, that'll be great. We'll be together forever!"

Patamon and his friend laughed.

Little did they know, on a small hill overlooking the village, Leomon watched them. He was close enough to hear every word.

Close enough to destroy them.

Part Two:
Legend of the
Digidestined

6

From the hilltop, Leomon could see all of Primary Village, and he had a perfect view of T.K. and his Digimon friend.

Slowly, the lion-faced Digimon Champion drew his long sword from his waist and growled, "I must obey the commands of Devimon."

Below him T.K. and Patamon were playing with a crowd of little digi-babies. "Hey, I know!" T.K. called out. "Let's play tag!"

Suddenly, all the baby Digimon stopped and cried out in surprise. T.K. frowned. "Well, okay, you don't have to play if—"

"T.K.!" Patamon cried in alarm. "Look!"

The boy glanced up to the hill that loomed

43

over them and gasped. Leomon was running down the hill at full speed, roaring something at them angrily. The babies scattered in all directions, but for a moment, T.K. was frozen in place.

Luckily, Patamon wasn't. As Leomon charged, the little Digimon let loose a Boom Bubble that landed square on Leomon's chest. The blast slowed Leomon down for a moment, but then he was back on his feet, rushing toward them.

But the delay had bought them some time. When Leomon reached the bottom of the hill, T.K. and Patamon had already dashed into the trees, looking for a place to hide.

Crouching behind a tree, Patamon and T.K. watched Leomon search through the forest. Patamon whispered, "Leomon used to be so nice. I wish we could get rid of the Black Gear that's controlling him!"

"That's easier said than done," T.K. whispered. "He's just too big."

"And what about me?" came a voice from behind them.

They looked around and found themselves staring up into the horrible face of Ogremon. He had followed Leomon and had managed to sneak up on them.

Ogremon laughed. "You're a nice little kid, aren't you? Too bad nice guys finish last!"

T.K. and Patamon scrambled away from Ogremon, but nearly ran right into the arms of Leomon. The fierce Digimon raised his blade. "I've been commanded to destroy you. I must obey!"

Patamon jumped in

front of T.K., but didn't know how he could protect the boy when he was such a small Digimon. *Why don't I digivolve?* he wondered. *What am I doing wrong?*

His question might never have been answered, for Leomon stalked forward, preparing to give the final blow. T.K. and Patamon looked around for some way to escape, but they were trapped by the two Evil Champions.

Just as the blade began to fall, they heard a distant voice roar, "Howling Blaster!"

Out of the woods streaked a bolt of blue-white energy. The energy beam zapped right toward Leomon, but the Digimon warrior managed to leap out of the way at the last minute.

"What's that?" Patamon wondered.

T.K. recognized the roar and the blast. "Look!"

Out of the forest charged a giant wolflike creature with a ring of feathers around his shoulders. On his back rode a boy a few years older than T.K. "That's my brother, Matt!" T.K. cheered.

"And he's with Garurumon!" Patamon added.

As the giant wolf Garurumon raced by, Matt jumped off and ran over to his brother. "T.K., are you all right?"

"Yes, I think so. Great to see you!" he said, giving his older brother a hug.

Garurumon, meanwhile, continued his charge toward Leomon. He let loose another Howling Blaster bolt, but this time Leomon blocked it with his sword. Leomon prepared to counterattack, but Garurumon was too fast for him. He covered the ground between them quickly and slammed his body into Leomon's. The fight was on.

Ogremon strode forward to join the fight, but found himself facing more kids and their Digimon. One of the kids, the boy called Tai, said, "You're not going anywhere."

"Oh," Ogremon laughed. "Is that what you say?"

"No," Tai admitted. "That's what he says." He pointed to someone behind Ogremon. "Get him, Greymon!"

T.K. didn't know where his friends had come from, or how they'd finally found him, but he was thrilled. Greymon gathered himself and cried, "Nova Blast!" as he let loose a powerful ball of fire. The blast missed Ogremon, but the explosion still tossed him a hundred feet away.

"Nice try!" Ogremon snarled. "You better

be careful playing with fire. Someone might get hurt. Namely me!"

Greymon unleashed another fireball, and this one scorched Ogremon's arms. "Well," he growled. "I'll just have to show you who's boss around here." He leaped at Greymon, who ducked under the blow. Ogremon laughed. "You're not so bad, I could fight you blindfol—*ooof!*"

He never finished his sentence as Greymon's tail swung around, slamming Ogremon back into the woods.

Nearby, Leomon and Garurumon fought to a standstill. Leomon's blade kept Garurumon at bay, but Garurumon's speed and strength prevented Leomon from escaping or attacking.

The fight looked like it could go on forever, until seven dark shapes appeared in the sky.

T.K. saw them first. "Watch out!" he called. "Black Gears!"

They all knew where the disks had come from. Devimon had sent them from Infinity

Mountain. The Digimon tensed, prepared to dodge them if the Black Gears came their way.

But the Gears weren't meant for them. They sailed right toward Leomon and plunged into his body. Leomon roared in agony, then continued to roar as an incredible change came over him. He began to grow.

"What's happening?" T.K. cried.

His brother, Matt, said, "Those Black Gears are turning him into a giant!"

7

In seconds, Leomon had grown to ten times his size, and now he towered over Garurumon. The wolflike Digimon growled, prepared to attack, but Leomon never gave him a chance. Thrusting his fist forward, Leomon summoned his Fist of the Beast King.

An energy bolt slammed into Garurumon, knocking the brave Digimon to the ground.

Without hesitating, Leomon sent another blast at Greymon, catching the Dinosaur Digimon off guard.

"No, we need you, Greymon!" Tai called.

Leomon heard a voice inside his head. *I command you to bring me the Digidestined, starting with the smallest child!* It was the voice of Devimon, urging him on.

In a menacing voice, Leomon replied, "I will obey you, Devimon."

The giant Digimon started forward, his eyes locked on T.K. With every enormous step he took, the ground trembled.

"T.K., watch out!" Matt cried.

But there was nowhere to go.

Patamon, small though he was, jumped between T.K. and the giant Leomon. "Boom Bubble!" he cried. The little energy bubble shot from his mouth but popped harmlessly against Leomon's massive chest. It didn't even slow him down.

Refusing to surrender, Patamon leaped into the air to attack Leomon, but the giant Digimon snatched him out of the air with one hand.

"Patamon!" T.K. called. Patamon could only gasp for breath as Leomon began to squeeze him.

But at that moment some of the other kids and their Digimon arrived.

Togemon, the cactus-shaped Digimon, slammed his full weight into Leomon. Strong as he was, Leomon could not hold on to Patamon, and dropped him.

"Patamon, are you okay?" T.K. said, running to his side.

Patamon lifted his head weakly. "I . . . I'm sorry. I was just trying to protect you."

"And you did great!" T.K. encouraged.

Nearby, others had arrived–Mimi, the computer brain Izzy and his Insectoid Digimon Kabuterimon, Sora with the firebirdlike Birdramon, Joe and his Digimon Ikkakumon.

Izzy jumped off Kabuterimon's back and called out, "Tai! I think I've found an answer!"

Tai glanced at Leomon, who would grab T.K. at any moment. "Then you'd better hurry!"

Izzy held up a small device—the same device they had all carried since they had been transported to File Island. It was about the size of a handheld game and seemed to be connected with the Digimon somehow. "It's the digivice, remember?" Izzy said. "We should try using it again!"

Tai nodded. None of them really understood the digivices yet, but they had used them to free Leomon from Devimon's power once before. It was worth another try.

Pulling out his own digivice, Tai ran toward Leomon, who now stood over T.K. as tall as a tower.

"Hey, you ready for a real fight?" Tai called. "Come on, booger breath, get me if you dare!"

Matt and T.K. both looked at Tai in complete surprise. "Dude, have you gone crazy?" Matt asked.

"Probably," Tai said, "but there's no other choice."

Leomon snarled. "I must have the Digidestined!"

He reached forward just as Tai reached him. Quick as lightning, Tai thrust his digivice

forward. As if it sensed the evil influence over Leomon, the digivice began to glow.

A brilliant light flared out of the device and washed over Leomon. The giant Digimon roared in pain and tried to cover his eyes.

Matt cheered and pulled out his own device. "These things pack quite a punch!" He jumped forward and raised his digivice, joining its power to Tai's.

Instantly, Leomon was surrounded by bright light. As the digivices' power washed over him, the Black Gears were driven out of his body.

They appeared over him, then faded away to wisps of darkness in the bright light.

Leomon himself collapsed to the ground.

Ogremon cried out in surprise. "How do those kids do that!"

"Hey, Ogremon!" Izzy cried. "Over here!"

Ogremon turned and saw Izzy and Kabuterimon. "You have not yet begun to feel our power!" Izzy yelled.

Then, Kabuterimon summoned his Electro Shocker. The lightning bolt struck Ogremon full on the chest and sent him flying out of sight.

The kids and their Digimon cheered. They rushed toward Leomon, who was slowly recovering from Devimon's evil influence.

As they gathered together, Ogremon watched them from the safety of the trees. "Ha!" he muttered. "Those fools don't know who they're dealing with. They're going to find out sooner than they think!"

Leomon sat beneath a tree to rest as he recovered his strength. The children and their Digimon gathered around him, and he explained to them the story of the Digidestined.

He said, "According to ancient legend, our world will be taken over by a strange, dark force that turns good Digimon into bad ones. Our ancestors believed that a group of children called the Digidestined would appear from another world. They would

possess superpowers that will eventually save our world from destruction. I believe the predictions have come true. File Island is in danger, and now you have appeared."

Tai said, "But how can you be sure we're the kids?"

Leomon pointed to the digivices they held. "It's been foretold that the Digidestined will have the ability to make Digimon digivolve. You've already done that."

"Wow," Matt said, impressed.

Izzy said, "I, for one, hope it's true. I believe that once we've achieved this goal we'll be able to leave File Island. Once our purpose is served, there'll be no other reason for us to remain."

Mimi perked up. "Then I'll finally be able to change these clothes!"

Matt scratched his head. "But how can we make it happen? We're not even sure who's causing it. What if it's a force that's too big for us to handle?"

Leomon uttered a growl low in his throat.

"Devimon is the main cause of the evil on this island. To stop it, you're going to have to defeat him."

There was a short silence as everyone considered how powerful Devimon was. But suddenly Tai jumped to his feet. "Let's go for it!" he said.

"What?" the others said at once.

Tai pointed up to Infinity Mountain. "Come on, everyone, why not? If we don't defeat him, this will never be over."

Izzy was the first to stand up beside him. "Yes, you're right. Besides, it's impossible for us to lose with the digivices."

The next to agree was Mimi, although for a totally different reason. "The first thing on

my list when we get home is to do some killer shopping!"

Agumon, Tai's Digimon friend who digivolved into Greymon, looked up at his companion. "I'm ready when you are, Tai!"

Gabumon grinned at his pal, Matt. "How about it, Matt, are we up to the challenge, my friend?"

Matt thought a moment, then nodded. "It's going to be tough. But when you get down to it, there's no other way."

Leomon looked proudly at the seven children and their Digimon. "All right, troops, let's get to it."

A short time later, a small boat left the chunk of island where Primary Village lay and drifted out into the open oceans of DigiWorld. In the boat sat Tai and Agumon, Matt and Gabumon, T.K. with Patamon, Mimi and Palmon, and Izzy with Tentomon. Leomon steered the boat, using his massive arms to

T.K. and Patamon crash-land!

Luckily, Primary Village is a total blast!

A fair tug-of-war battle between Patamon and Elecmon cools their Digimon tempers.

It's always better to have friends
than enemies . . .

. . . because in DigiWorld,
danger is never far away.

Not again! Leomon is infected by a triple dose of Black Gears.

Digivice power!

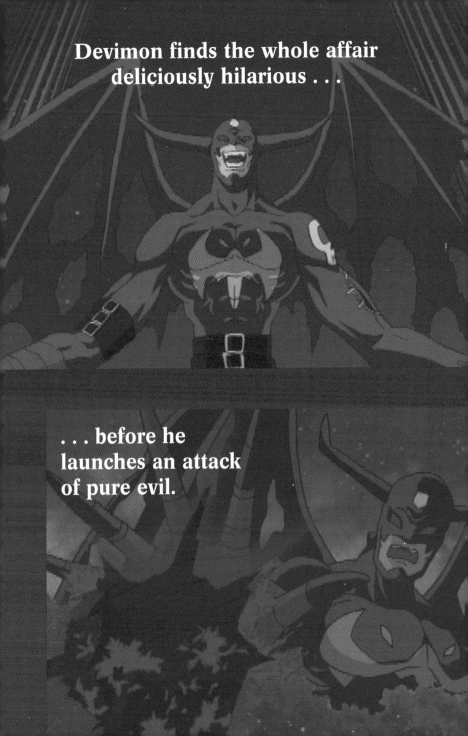

Devimon finds the whole affair
deliciously hilarious . . .

. . . before he
launches an attack
of pure evil.

Patamon
digvolve to . . .

. . . Angemon!

The ultimate battle of good versus evil.

Even though T.K. will miss his good friend, the Digidestined won this round . . .

. . . but will Devimon have the last laugh?

row the small boat across the choppy waters of the sea.

The children watched as Infinity Mountain drew nearer. With every passing moment, it seemed to rise higher and higher into the sky. No one spoke as they approached the rocky shores of that broken bit of island, and when they all set foot on dry land, each of them felt a twinge of fear. They were going to face the most powerful—and the most evil—of all the Digimon.

From the heights of the mountain, Devimon looked down on them and smiled. "They're being led here by that traitor Leomon. Even after breaking free of my power, he continues to be very valuable to me."

Ogremon snorted. "Maybe, but I'm better looking."

Devimon scowled. "And you will be useful, Ogremon. You will pay them one final visit."

Without warning, Devimon reached out with one long skeletal hand and touched Ogremon.

Instantly, the Digimon was gone, replaced by a swarm of the dangerous Black Gears. For an instant, the Black Gears hung in the air. Then they zipped away, cutting across the sky like dark blades.

Devimon laughed. "Hear this, Digidestined!

I am the supreme master of this island. My power is infinite!"

Near the other side of the Infinity Mountain island, two more Digimon were making their way toward land. Joe's Digimon had already digivolved into the powerful walruslike Ikkakumon, while Sora's Bird Digimon had digivolved into fiery Birdramon. Because they could cross the ocean without a boat, they'd split up, attempting to take Devimon by surprise.

But as Ikkakumon swam and Birdramon soared above him, they saw a cloud of dark objects gathering over the mountain. Then the dark cloud formed a stream that flowed right toward the peak.

"Black Gears!" said Joe, clinging to giant Ikkakumon's neck. "What are they doing?"

Sora, who was sitting on one of Birdramon's talons as the Digimon flew, said, "It's like Devimon's gathering all his power."

"This is going to be the big one, Joe," Ikkakumon said. "It's time to show what you're really made of."

Joe, who had never been the bravest of the children, nodded. "We'd better hurry and catch up to the others."

On land, the first group of children had climbed halfway up the mountain. At Infinity's peak, they could see an ancient building squatting under a dark cloud.

It doesn't look so bad, Tai thought. *Maybe Devimon won't put up much of a fight after all.*

He couldn't have been more wrong.

A moment later, the entire mountain began to tremble. Rocks tumbled down the mountainside, first as a trickle of pebbles, then as a rain of boulders crashing down around them.

"Look up there!" Matt cried.

All eyes went to the peak, where Devimon's fortress sat. There was a loud crash, the sound of cracking rock, and then the top blew off the fortress.

Up rose Devimon like a giant stretching out of a tiny house.

The children had seen giant Digimon before, but never had they seen anything like Devimon as he now appeared. He was bigger than a house, bigger even than a small hill. He rose up like a mountain standing on top of a mountain. His black wings stretched so wide they nearly blocked out the sun.

Devimon looked down on them and laughed.

9

The children looked up at Devimon and their jaws dropped in surprise.

Palmon shivered. "I ... I didn't expect him to be such a big guy."

Izzy said, "Just like a bad guy. They always think bigger is better."

"Don't underestimate him," Leomon growled. They all looked at him. Even he, a

Champion of the good Digimon, looked nervous standing there in the shadow of Devimon. "His power is immense. So be careful."

Devimon flapped his massive wings and launched himself into the sky, looming over them like a storm cloud. The children and their Digimon could only watch in fear as the devilish monster drifted slowly down. As he planted his feet on the ground near them, the whole world seemed to shake.

"Um, Agumon," Tai said. "You'd better digivolve."

The little Digimon gulped. "Uh, yeah, you're right!"

Devimon turned to face them. He was so big that just the turn of his body and the movement of one giant wing caused a great wind that nearly blew everyone off their feet.

Without a word, the evil Digimon raised one hand. Black light burst forth and slammed against the children and their Digital Monsters. It was the power of pure evil, and it crashed down on them like a shower of stones. Even Leomon could not stand up to its power.

But Devimon had forgotten all the Digimon. He'd been so eager to destroy them in one fell swoop, he had not counted their number—not until the voice of Ikkakumon cried from behind him. "Harpoon Torpedo!"

Devimon turned just in time to see the Digimon Champion launch rockets from his horned head. The rockets rose, then broke into a dozen smaller torpedoes, all flying

toward Devimon. Even that powerful creature could not avoid them in time, and the torpedoes blasted against his chest, knocking him backward.

"Bull's-eye!" Joe cheered.

The Digimon did not let up. Birdramon flapped her wings and fired her Meteor Wing attack. For a moment, Devimon disappeared behind a wall of fire.

Sora ran to the others. "Everyone, there's no time to waste. We've got to strike right away."

Tai looked at little Agumon. "Digivolve!"

"You got it!" Agumon said. "Agumon digivolve to . . . Greymon!"

With a flash of light, the small dinosaur was replaced by the mighty Digimon Champion known as Greymon—a massive *Tyrannosaurus rex* with a horned helmet on his head.

Next came Matt's companion. "Gabumon digivolve to . . . Garurumon!" And there stood the giant wolf, who let loose a fierce growl.

One by one, the Digimon digivolved into powerful Champions.

"Tentomon digivolve to . . . Kabuterimon!"

"Palmon digivolve to . . . Togemon!" and Mimi's plantlike friend was replaced by the giant cactus creature.

Now all the Digimon that could digivolve had transformed from Rookies into Champions, and they wasted no time attacking.

"Nova Blast!"

"Howling Blaster!"

Garurumon and Greymon hit Devimon together. The blows seemed to stun the evil creature for a moment, and Garurumon charged forward, clamping his jaws around Devimon's arm.

"I think he's got him," Tai said.

But Devimon snapped his arm, and Garurumon could not hold on. He hurtled

through the air and smashed into Greymon, crushing them both against a rock wall.

"You'll have to try harder than that!" Devimon laughed.

"Electro Shocker!" shouted Kabuterimon, flapping his insect wings and taking flight.

"Needle Spray!" called Togemon.

Lightning bolts and razor-sharp spears flew at Devimon, but the Evil Digimon brushed them off. He pushed Togemon aside and them swatted Kabuterimon out of the sky.

"Oh, no!" Mimi called out.

Now it was Leomon's turn to join the action. With a mighty leap he threw himself at Devimon's back. But out of nowhere appeared Ogremon, hidden by some spell of Devimon's. Ogremon met Leomon in midair, stopping him from striking Devimon. As Leomon recovered from the collision of bodies, Devimon turned and saw him. He released another blast of evil power and hit Leomon like a battering ram. Leomon was carried a hundred yards through the air and vanished into a grove of trees.

Birdramon swooped down for another strike, but this time Devimon was waiting for her. With his gigantic arms, he snatched her out of the sky and held her tight as though she were nothing more than a baby bird.

"You're not worth my time!" he said. "Get out of my sight!"

He threw her at Greymon, who was just recovering from the first round, and the two Digimon fell to the ground.

Devimon turned to Ikkakumon. Ikkakumon roared and fired more Harpoon Torpedoes. But Devimon was faster. He reached out and plucked Ikkakumon off the ground and used him as a club to strike Kabuterimon. When they fell, not a single Digimon was left standing.

Except for Patamon. The tiny Digimon Rookie stood next to T.K. Unable to digi-

volve, Patamon had not joined the fight of Champions.

"Now for you," Devimon said. "The legends say the smallest shall destroy me. I'm not going to let that happen."

The giant arm reached down to crush T.K. and Patamon, and all they could do was watch.

At the last moment, a blur of blue and

white flashed past them, crashing into Devimon's arm. It was Garurumon! The wolflike Digimon's jaws bit into Devimon's wrist like a vise and the evil monster roared in pain.

Before Devimon could strike back against Garurumon, Greymon grabbed his ankle and bit down hard.

Ikkakumon followed, and so did Kabuterimon, and Birdramon, and Togemon. With the last of their strength, the Champion Digimon grabbed hold of Devimon to keep him from harming T.K. and Patamon.

The gigantic Devimon roared in anger and pain. Through gritted fangs, he said, "You seem to forget. I am Devimon. I have power over all Digimon. You cannot defeat me!"

With that, Devimon unleashed his most powerful blow. The black light of his evil strength flew outward in all directions like an explosion, blowing the Digimon away from him.

Even the strongest of them could not

resist. The six Digimon hit the ground and could not move.

"Now," said Devimon, reaching for T.K., "it ends."

10

Patamon saw Devimon reach for them. He wished he could digivolve, but nothing happened.

But he knew he had to protect T.K. He flew into the air and fired a Boom Bubble. It broke uselessly against Devimon's gigantic hand. If Garurumon's Howling Blaster and Greymon's Nova Blast could not defeat Devimon, how could little Patamon?

"Why can't I digivolve!" he cried.

Devimon had almost reached T.K. "Patamon, help!"

Desperate, Patamon did the only thing he could. He threw himself between Devimon and T.K.

The evil monster's hand closed around Patamon.

Devimon smiled. He would simply crush the Digimon first, then the boy.

But as Devimon squeezed his fist to destroy the creature, he found he could not do it. In fact, he suddenly felt like he was holding a flame–the little Digimon had turned white-hot! Brilliant beams of light burst from between his fingertips.

Nearby, Matt saw what was happening. "It's Patamon. He's digivolving at last!"

Devimon tried to hold on, but the power was too great even for him. His fingers flew open, and the white light nearly blinded him.

He let go and staggered back as Patamon completed his transformation.

"Patamon digivolve to . . . Angemon!"

The creature that stood before them was tall and white, with three sets of beautiful white wings and a staff of gold. A helmet covered his head.

Though smaller than Devimon, Angemon shone with a brilliance that cut through Devimon's darkness.

"Wow," said Tai, "that little guy really had it in him."

But Devimon wasn't afraid. "What's this, another foolish attempt?"

Angemon, hovering in the sky, looked down at the evil creature. "The forces of good are more powerful. Even you can't stop us. I have come to destroy you and bring peace to the island."

Angemon raised his staff.

But instead of firing a blast, the staff seemed to soak in power. The digivices of

all seven children flared brightly, and beams of light shot out and struck the staff.

In seconds, it glowed brighter than the sun.

"I won't let you take my power away!" Devimon roared. "I'll fight you to the end!"

Angemon looked unafraid. "If I can help others, my fate is unimportant."

Devimon reached forward. Angemon seemed to wait for him, calmly, patiently. Just as the evil creature was about to strike, Angemon raised his fist. It glowed with all the power Angemon had gathered.

Then, at the last moment, the glowing Digimon punched his hand forward. The power he unleashed was like nothing the others had ever seen. A shaft of pure white light punched right through Devimon, who cried out in surprise. A ball of fire exploded outward from Angemon in all directions, completely covering Devimon.

The evil creature screamed and started to break into a million scattered pieces. But even as he did, he snarled at Angemon. "You've used all your power in one blow. Not very wise of you! That means you'll be

destroyed along with me. And there are other Digimon, some even more powerful than I am, who'll take my place. You haven't won at all!"

Then Devimon vanished, ripped apart by Angemon's power.

The angel-like creature himself began to fade, as though the effort to put forth so much power was draining him.

"Angemon!" T.K. cried out. "Where are you going?"

"T.K.," Angemon said gently. "I'll come back, if you want me to." Then he was gone, disappearing into the blinding white light that was all around them.

In a moment, the light, too, began to fade.

T.K. blinked. When his eyes cleared, he saw that a Digi-Egg had been left at his feet. T.K. picked it up. "Do you think . . . do you think this could be Angemon?"

Gabumon smiled. "I know it is. He's just resting."

Palmon nodded. "Don't worry. You'll see him again when he digivolves."

Sora said, "Hey, look!" She pointed out to the sea. Huge pieces of the broken island were drifting back toward Infinity Mountain. Piece by piece, the island was coming back together.

"Exactly," Izzy said. "Now that evil has been defeated, the island is returning to its normal state."

Matt shook his head. "But what about those other evil Digimon that Devimon mentioned. Do we have to fight them, too?"

"I thought we were going home," Joe said.

"I don't want to fight anymore," Mimi said. "I think I broke a nail."

Tai said, "Well, we've got to do it. If that's what it takes to get home, we'll defeat all the evil in this world. After all, according to Leomon's legend, we're the Digidestined!"

Write Your Own Digimon Story!

Fill out the blank spaces according to the cues given below. On the following page, your answers will be used to create a story about your own adventure in DigiWorld. Don't look at the story on the next page yet, because that will spoil the fun of seeing your hilarious story before it's finished.

A silly name: _____.

Name of a town: _____.

Name of a game or sport: _____.

Name of your best friend: _____.

A color: _____.

A natural disaster (example: "tornado"): _____.

A foreign country: _____.

Your favorite Digimon character from Season 2:

_____.

An enthusiastic, silly greeting (example: "Whazzup!"):

_____.

A noun (A noun is a person, place, or thing, like, "rock."):

_____.

Another noun: _____.

A type of weather (example: "rainy"): _____.

A noun: _____.

Type of animal: _____.

Name of a scary Digimon: _____.

Body part (example: "arm"): _____.

A noun: _____.

A body of water (example: "lake"): _____.

An emotion (examples: "happy" or "confused"):

_____.

A noun: _____.

Type of clothing: _____.

An exclamation (example: "Look out!"): _____.

A noun: _____.

Your school: _____.

My Day in DigiWorld
By _____
1.

You'll never believe what happened to me. I was hanging out one summer day in _____,
2.

playing _____ with _____ .
3.   4.

All of a sudden, the sky turned _____ and a
5.

huge _____ hit and carried us off to
6.

DigiWorld. I thought we were in _____ until I
7.

saw _____ . He came up and said,
8.

"_____." We started walking through

       9.

DigiWorld, checking out all the Digi-_____ and

                                 10.

Digi-_____. It was really _____ outside,

      11.   12.

so we decided to just play around and throw

_____(s) at each other. But just when I forgot

  13.

about my pet _____ back home and started

               14..

thinking I would stay in DigiWorld forever,

_____ showed up. He growled at us and

      15.

showed us his terrible _____. He used his

                        16.

scary Digi-_____ against us, pushing us slowly

        17.

toward the _____. That's when I really

         18.

started to feel _____, because I can't

           19.

swim! We had to do something quick.

      Luckily, with the help of the Crest of Knowledge
and the Digi-Egg of _____, the

                    20.

tide of the battle started to change. I noticed the
digivice attached to my _____, and I used
                              21.
it to help my Digimon friend digivolve. Then I yelled,
"_____," to distract the enemy, and all
        22.
three of us started kicking some Digi-Butt! Finally, our
evil Digimon opponent gave up and ran away.

        Our adventure was over and it was time for me
to go home. I told my new friend he was a real
_____ , and that he should come visit
        23.
me sometime. I sure hope that he does, because I want
to show him off to my friends at _____ .
                                        24.

Check out these other cool
Digimon Digital Monsters™ books
from HarperEntertainment!

Digimon Digital Monsters™ :
MAP OF FILE ISLAND
By J. E. Bright

Digimon Digital Monsters™ :
THE OFFICIAL GAME GUIDE
By John Whitman

Digimon Digital Monsters™ :
THE OFFICIAL CHARACTER GUIDE
By A. Ryan Nerz

Coming Soon:

Digimon Digital Monsters™ :
THE QUEST FOR CRESTS
By J. E. Bright

Digimon Digital Monsters™
2nd Season Ultimate Adventures #1:
DIGIARMOR ENERGIZE!
By Lisa Papademetriou